JUNGLE MUSIC IS A SOUND SYSTEM CULTURE, CRAFTED IN THE EARLY 90s - FOLLOWING THE UK BREAKBEAT/HARDCORE SCENE, FUSING DRUM MACHINES, SYNTHESISERS & SAMPLING DUB, REGGAE, FUNK, SOUL & ANYTHING THE PRODUCERS COULD GET THEIR HANDS ON AT THE TIME!

THIS IS ONE OF THE UK'S LONGEST LIVED SUB-CULTURES, ARGUABLY THE COUNTRY'S LARGEST & MOST ORIGINAL MUSICAL EXPORT, WHICH PACKS OUT NIGHTCLUBS & VENUES ALL OVER THE GLOBE EVERY WEEK!

THIS BOOK TOUCHES ON SOME THE MOST IMPORTANT LABELS RESPONSIBLE FOR THE SCENE'S FOUNDATIONS - ALONG WITH SOME RARE, HARD TO FIND & MORE RECENT LABELS THAT ARE KEEPING THE JUNGLIST MOVEMENT ROLLING ON...

Words
Lewis Joyce (Sicknote)
& Chris Dexta

Editor
Colin Steven

Design
Banan Gun

Publishers
Southside Circulrs
& Velocity Press

Originally printed
August 2022

Third edition
October 2024

southsidecirculars.com
velocitypress.uk

VP023

ISBN: 978-1-913231-40-8

THE ICON CATALOGUE
JUNGLE
VOL. 1

01. 3AM ETERNAL
02. 3RD EYE
03. ARMHOUSE CREW
04. CODE-001
05. CONQUEROR
06. DOPE DRAGON
07. DREAD
08. DROPPIN' SCIENCE
09. FORMATION
10. FRESH 86
11. GANJA
12. IBIZA RECORDS
13. IN TOUCH
14. INTALEX
15. IQ RECORDS
16. KEMET
17. KUTE KUTZ
18. LEGEND
19. LUCKY SPIN
20. MASK RECORDS
21. MOVING SHADOW
22. MYOR MASSIV
23. NO U-TURN
24. OKBRON
25. RAM RECORDS
26. REDSKIN
27. REINFORCED
28. ROUGH TONE
29. RUDEBOY RECORDS
30. RUGGED VINYL
31. RUPTURE LONDON
32. SOAPBAR
33. SPLASH
34. SUB ASSERTAIVE SOUNDS
35. SUBLIMINAL
36. UNDERWORLD VINYL
37. URBAN GORILLIA
38. V RECORDINGS
39. WESTERN LORE
40. WHITE HOUSE

3AM ETERNAL

2020 - PRESENT

One of the new wave Jungle labels, run by Rotterdam based FFF, bringing in the new generation whilst fueling the oldskool heads with the junglist fire they crave! Cuts from Coco Bryce, Duburban & Artificial Red

THE ESSENTIALS

FFF 'CAN'T SAY NO'

ARTIFICIAL RED 'MYSTICS'

3RD EYE

1994

Home to some of the earliest Photek productions, under the alias System X. Only three releases on this imprint, but have become super saught after.. Get your credit cards out - these ones are expensive!

THE ESSENTIALS

SYSTEM X 'SAY IT'

SYSTEM X 'METAMORPHASIS'

ARMSHOUSE CREW RECORDS

1992 - 1995

Lennie De Ice's label, featuring the reissue and remixes of 'We Are I.E' - also home to his colaborations with a very young d-Bridge, and music from the Dreem Teems Timmi Magic!

THE ESSENTIALS

DUBB HUSTLERS 'THE POISON EP'

LENNIE DE ICE 'MY HOOD'

CODE-001

1994 - 1995

Sister label to Inivisible Man's 'Legend' label. With only 3 releases to its name, this side project didn't last too long but was home to the debut release of Oxfords very own Mouley & Lucidia!

THE ESSENTIALS

MOUL'E & LUCIDA 'CITY IN THE CLOUDS'
THE INVISIBLE MAN 'SKY LINER (95 VIP)'

CONQUEROR

1994 - 1996

One of Kickin Records' many sub labels, focusing on the Ragga Jungle style. Conqueror was short lived but packed a punch with choice cuts from the likes of Dillinja, Lemon D and XTC

THE ESSENTIALS

DILLINJA 'TEAR DOWN (DA WHOLE PLACE)'

LEMON D 'JAH LOVE'

DOPE DRAGON

1995 - 1998 / 2005 - 2006

Full Cycle's sister label leaning towards the more Jump-up style of Jungle. With label crew representing under aliases, bringing a raw and nasty side to their sound. This offshoot is not to be overlooked!

THE ESSENTIALS

GANG RELATED & MASK 'SOLDIER'
RONI SIZE & KRUST 'SELEKTOR BWOY (KRUST MIX)'

DREAD

1995 - PRESENT

The home of Ray Keith and his many aliaes; THE Terrosit, Babylon 5 & Armegedon. Releasing a whole load of anthems & music from Dillinja & Lemon D and productions by BLADERUNNER, Twisted Anger and John Rolodex.

THE ESSENTIALS

THE TERRORIST 'SING TIME'
THE TERRORIST 'THE CHOPPER'

DROPPIN' SCIENCE

1993 - 2002

Label set-up by Danny Breaks, mainly for his own productions, but also featured early works from the likes of Mark Pritchard, Dylan, Fracture & Neptune... Pretty much every release on this label is gold!

THE ESSENTIALS

DANNY BREAKS 'DROPPIN' SCIENCE VOL.1'
VERTIGO 'THE DRAINED'

FORMATION

1991 - PRESENT

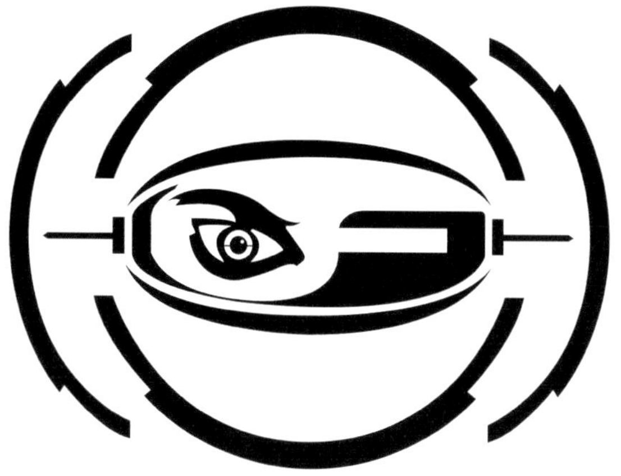

DJ SS's label, born in the Hardcore era, but at the forefront of the Jungle movement - with an arsenal of anthems and a long list of VIPs touching down over the years - check the back catalog for a real history lesson!

THE ESSENTIALS

SOUND OF THE FUTURE 'THE LIGHTER'
MA2 'HEARING IS BELIEVING'

FRESH 86

1995 - 1998 / 2014 - PRESENT

TOM REDEYE's label showcasing early Digital & Spirit (R.I.P) music, highlighting talent in his hometown: Ipswich. The 2nd phase came during the Jungle resurgance with releaese from Threshold, Kid Lib, Coco Bryce & more!

THE ESSENTIALS

THE SPIRIT 'THE RIFF'

THEORY 'AMAZON'

GANJA

1994 - 1996 / 2003 - 2011

DJ Hypes first record label. Raw, hard hitting Ragga Jungle & Jump-up weapons from Hype himself, DJ Zinc & Pascal (aka. Ganja Krew) and remixes from some of the heavyweights of the time; Dextrous, Smokey Joe & T-Bone.

THE ESSENTIALS

THE GANJA KRU 'TIGER STYLE'

DJ ZINC 'SUPER SHARP SHOOTER'

IBIZA

1990 - 2000 / 2017 - PRESENT

Another label that set the foundations of the scene and pushed the sound from the early Hardcore days and then into the Jungle realm, Noise factory and Potential Bad Boy coming with the goods early on here!

THE ESSENTIALS

NOISE FACTORY 'FEEL THE RUSH'
POTENTIAL BAD BOY 'NEW STYLE'

IN TOUCH

1992 - 1997

IN TOUCH
RECORDS

Mike De Underground's label, mostly a home to early releases by his brother Pete (aka. Cool Hand Flex) - but also tracks from Blue Zone, Hopa & Bones, aswell as Mike himself under his Mikey-D pseudonym..

THE ESSENTIALS

COOL HAND FLEX 'MELODY MADNESS'

HOPA & BONES 'ALI BA-BA'

INTALEX

1995 - 1996

Manchester based label started by Mark XTC & Marcus Intalex with early works from themselves, as well as music from THE OUTLAW and Manchester legends Sappo & ST Files (who went on to form Soul:R with Marcus)

THE ESSENTIALS

DA INTALEX 'MERCY'

THE OUTLAW 'O.G. CALL'

IQ RECORDS

1994 - 1996

Started by DJ Sponge and featuring early Jungle heaters from Dillinja, Fallen Angel (Wax Doctor & Alex Resse) and Mareveous CAIN. Has recently started reissuing some of the back catalogue via Ibiza Records!

THE ESSENTIALS

DILLINJA '3:01 IN THE MORNING'

FALLEN ANGELS 'HELLO LOVER (BASS / HEAVY MIX)

KEMET

1992 - 1997 / 2001 - 2008 / 2016 - PRESENT

Tottenham based label from Mark Ranger. Fundimental in the early days of the Hardcore Jungle sound, also responsible for the 3rd Party sub-label & many classic reissues that are coming thick & fast!

THE ESSENTIALS

BRAIN KILLERS 'SCREWFACE'
NOISE FACTORY 'BREAKAGE #4'

KUTE KUTZ

1994 - 1995

Only two releases on this label, both by the elusive Maytrix, but certainly worth the mention; especialy the first release which is most likely in every Jungle heads' wantlist! Soulful / Ragga Jungle at it's finest..

THE ESSENTIALS

DA MAYTRIX 'LET ME KNOW'

DA MAYTRIX 'THE RIDE'

LEGEND

1993 - 1996

Originaly started by Invisibale man & Gwange, later handed to Q project & SpinbacK - the label went on to release some serious heavyeight classics. Early releases are now super saught after, and for good reason!

THE ESSENTIALS

LEE & TANGO 'SOLUTIONS'

Q PROJECT 'CHAMPION SOUND'

LUCKY SPIN

1992 - 1996

LUCKY SPIN
RECORDINGS

Run out of the Lucky Spin shop - they released early productions from Orca (Decoder), DJ Trace & Voyager and had pete parson on the buttons in the studio situated next door. Powerhouse of a label!

THE ESSENTIALS

DJ TRACE 'LOST ENTITY (REMIX)'

ORCA 'INTALECT'

MASK RECORDS

1993 - 1994

Highly overlooked label, some proper early Dark Jungle from Love Dove Jay, heavy artillery for any hardcore junglists. Revived in '96 as a more D&B imprint along with name change to Mask Productions.

THE ESSENTIALS

LOVE DOVE JAY 'FINAL SOLUTION'

JUGIER 'SHES DEAD BY NOW'

MOVING SHADOW

1990 - 2006

One of the most important labels in the Jungle universe.. With the A&R help of 2-Bad-Mice, Rob Playford's label is responsible for tonnes of careers, timeless classics & anthems! Also had a radio station on GTA3!

THE ESSENTIALS

OMNI TRIO 'RENEGADE SNARES (FOUL PLAY REMIX)'
FOUL PLAY 'BEING WITH YOU'

MYOR MASSIV

2015 - PRESENT

The Jungle / Hardcore arm of Coco Bryce's MYOR empire, featuring some of the modern Jungle heavyweights such as FFF, Tim Reaper & Kid Lib - pushing for modern production dipped in old school styles.

THE ESSENTIALS

COCO BRYCE 'LOVIN U'
KID LIB 'FALLING'

NO U-TURN

1994 - 2006

Noted as one of the labels that started the Tech-Step sound & movement, but also known for some absoulte Jungle belters from the likes of DJ Buz, Ed Rush, Gunshot,DJ Kane & DJ Ruffkut - run by Nico.

THE ESSENTIALS

DJ BUZ 'WATCH ME NOW'

ED RUSH 'THE FORCE IS ELECTRIC (REMIX)'

OKBRON

2019 - PRESENT

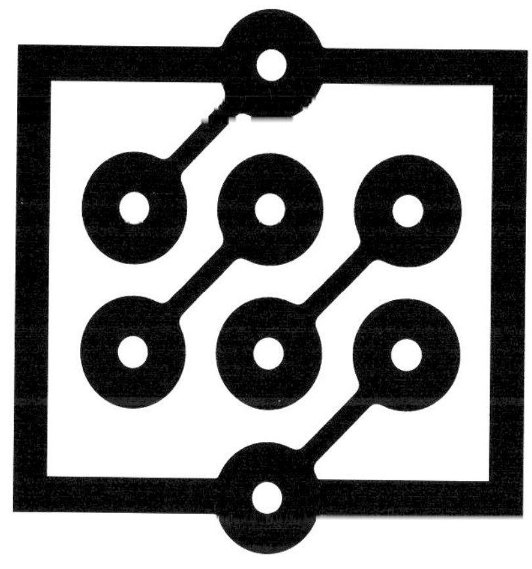

Russian based Okbron have been providing us with some well deserved unreleased gems from the Speed era. To date - tunes from Axis, Big Bud, Krust & PFM, alongside new music from Bungle, DJ Trax, Response & Pliskin.

THE ESSENTIALS

FORME 'IN YOUR DREAMS'

G FORCE 'PROXIMITY (ASC REMIX)'

RAM RECORDS

1992 - PRESENT

Founded in 1992 by Andy C, with Ant Miles & Red-One, RAM was at the forefront of Jungle's formation and went on to be a majour player and one of the biggest and most recognised labels in the D&B world.

THE ESSENTIALS

ANDY C 'ROLL ON'

ORIGIN UNKNOWN 'VALLEY OF THE SHADOWS'

REDSKIN

1992 - 1995

Label run by Neil Redskin, super sought after early Ragga Jungle artillery which in recent years have started to be reissued due to high demand! Orginal copies still fetch big money on the old “Skalpers Paradise”.

THE ESSENTIALS

CHATTA B 'NOTCH'

STUDIO II 'ENTERTAINMENT'

REINFORCED

1990 - PRESENT

The R! Setting foundations for so much of what we listen to today in Jungle / D&B, Reinforced is a seminal label, all you need to do is look at there back catalogue to see what they have done for the scene.

THE ESSENTIALS

NOOKIE 'ONLY YOU'

TEK 9 'DEM A GWAN LIKE DEM KNOW BADNESS'

ROUGH TONE

1992 - 1995

Setup in 1992 by E.Q.P (Earl Falconer of UB40, alongside Patrick Tenyue & Gerry Parchment) as a home for their music. Classics from DJ Ron & DJ Nut Nut, and early productions by Mark Caro (Tech Itch)

THE ESSENTIALS

DJ RON 'MO MUSIK (AFRICAN CHANT MIX)'
DJ RON & E.Q.P. 'CRACKMAN THE RETURN (DJ RON RMX)'

RUDEBOY RECORDS

1992 - 1994

'Early Breakbeat Techno' label from Rob Solomon featuring mainly his collaborations with Rupert Parks (Photek) under the name Origination - super rare, and cost an arm and leg if you do come across them...

THE ESSENTIALS

ORIGINATION 'SIGNAL TO NOISE'

ORIGINATION 'MAKE YA WANNA DO RIGHT'

RUGGED VINYL

1992 - 2002

Started by Ben James & Ray Stanley (D.O.P.E) - originally releasing their own music alongside SMF releases rugged developed focusing more on the Inteligent Jungle sound with music from the likes of Intense!

THE ESSENTIALS

D.O.P.E 'TRAVELLING PT 2'

INTENSE 'THE DREAMER'

RUPTURE LONDON

2012 - PRESENT

One of London's most exciting and forward thinking Jungle / D&B club nights, run by Mantra & Double O; has gone on to become a buy on sight label. Showcasing artists that play the night and the sounds they supply!

THE ESSENTIALS

DOUBLE O 'BLACKULA'

FOREST DRIVE WEST 'JUNGLE CRACK'

SOAPBAR

1992 - 1994

Set up by Total Music (record shop) & A&R headed by DJ Spice. Featuring music from T.Power, Cris B and the Ray Keith remix of MOBY which became 'Yes Yes'. Their vinyl output has now reached golddust status!

THE ESSENTIALS

JOINT PROJECT 'TOTAL FEELING'

CRIS B 'MIND BODY & SOUL'

SPLASH

1994 - 2001

Originally started by Daz (Undercover Agent) and later merged with Juice Recordings. Released some absolute killers, leaning on the more jump-up side, outliving the Jungle era moving into the D&B realm!

THE ESSENTIALS

UNDERCOVER AGENT 'BARRACUDA'

SPLASH COLLECTIVE 'REBELS'

SUB ASSERTIVE SOUNDS

1994

Ragga Jungle focused label based in Birmingham, associated with events QDance & B9. Run by Calvin Sheppard - with releases from Dubtronics (Jeremy Sylvester), Darkus & Amp, G E Real.

THE ESSENTIALS

DUBTRONIX FEAT G E REAL 'KILL SOME SOUNDS'

THE URBAN TRIBE 'UNTITLED A'

SUBLIMINAL

1992 - 1993

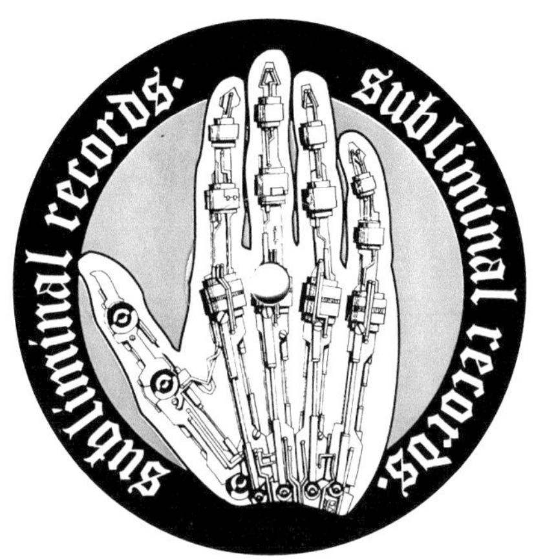

Very shortlived label with only three releases under the belt, all from Intense's White House Crew & Baylon Timewarp collaborations - Hardcore Jungle slammers which will require a dip into the savings..

THE ESSENTIALS

THE WHITE HOUSE CREW 'ANONYMOUS'

BABYLON TIMEWARP 'DURBAN POISON (NUT-E-1 REMIX)'

UNDERWORLD VINYL

1994

Only two releases on this label but both absoulte killers and know fetching big bucks on the second hand market.. Top class Jungle weaonary from On Remand, Veritgo, with remix work from the late Tango (R.I.P)

THE ESSENTIALS

ON REMAND 'CONTROLLIN (TANGO REMIX)
VERTIGO 'CHEMICAL WARFARE'

URBAN GORILLA

1995 - 1997

Part of the Public Demand label group, original output all on the Jungle tip - featuring tunes from DJ Rap, Ray Keith, Steve Gurley plus many others.. Reformed in 2002 as a full on UK Garage imprint!

THE ESSENTIALS

DR S GACHET & AUDIO MAZE 'DREAMER (NOOKIE RMX)

DJ RAP MEETS DA B.O.S.S. 'IM SO?'

V RECORDINGS

1993 - PRESENT

Yet another foundation label for the scene. Run by Bryan G & Jumping Jack Frost the label has released many anthems over the years and is firmly rooted in the history books of Jungle / Drum & Bass!

THE ESSENTIALS

DJ KRUST 'BURNING'

LEMON D 'I CANT STOP'

WESTERN LORE

2017 - PRESENT

Modern Jungle imprint from Bristol based Alex Eveson (aka Dead Man's Chest), showcasing the more rugged / experimental new gen artists, such as Response & Pliskin, Crypticz, Eusebeia & Artificial Red.

THE ESSENTIALS

DEAD MAN'S CHEST 'JUST 4'

RESPONSE & PLISKIN 'BUREAUCRACY'

WHITE HOUSE

1992 - 1998

White house ran out of Mo Musics Machine was another crucial label from the early days of Jungle - releasing early works from the likes of Skanna, Remarc, The Criminal Minds, Justice & Bizzy B.

THE ESSENTIALS

BIZZY B 'M.C. MENTAZM'

JUSTICE & MERCY 'SOOTHE MY SOUL'

SOUTHSIDECIRCULARS.COM